MOVING

by

Bernard Slade

SAMUEL FRENCH, INC.

45 West 25th Street   7623 Sunset Boulevard
NEW YORK 10010   HOLLYWOOD 90046
LONDON   *TORONTO*

IMPORTANT BILLING AND CREDIT REQUIREMENTS

All producers of **MOVING** must give credit to the Author of the Play in all programs distributed in connection with performances of the Play, and in all instances in which the title of the Play appears for the purposes of advertising, publicizing or otherwise exploiting the Play and /or a production. The name of the Author must appear on a separate line on which no other name appears, immediately following the title and must appear in size of type not less than fifty percent of the size of the title type.

CAST
(in order of appearance)

BARBARA HARTMAN— Forties, attractive, feminine.

MILDRED WRIGHT — A large, handsome, ageless black woman, probably in her sixties.

FRED SAPSTEAD — Barbara's father. A spry, very young man in his late seventies.

TIMMY HARTMAN — Barbara's fifteen year old son, studious, bright.

HARRY PICARDO — Overweight Italian mover in his late fifties.

JOEY PICARDO — Harry's son, in his early twenties, lithely built, must dance a little.

CHARLIE HARTMAN — Barbara's ex-husband, a charming, boyish man in his forties.

JENNIFER HARTMAN — Barbara's twenty year old daughter, Tomboyish, athletic.

LISA — The fifteen year old girl from next door.

MAVIS CRUIKSHANK — A ditsy, overblown real estate woman.

HILARY HARTMAN — Barbara's twenty-four year old daughter.

ACT I

(THE TIME: The present. 6:30 A.M. Of an early October day.
THE SETTING: Two stories of a charming, beautiful, old Victorian
house in Greenwich, Connecticut. The living room dominates a
soaring unit set with the Downstage apron and side spill of the
stage being used for scenes played outside the house. The front
door into the living room and an entrance to the kitchen are
visible and some French doors and a large window on the Up-
stage wall enable us to get an impression of a heavily treed
back garden. Stairs ascend to a landing that overlooks the liv-
ing room. Outside, a portion of a moveable Victorian gazebo is
in evidence. The house play should give the overall impression
of a substantial, unique, rather eccentric residence that, although
furnished with a blend of present and past, nostalgically speaks
to us of a gentle, gracious bygone era. When the audience en-
ters the theatre the curtain is up but the set is concealed by a
scrim covered with enlarged, faded snapshots of the members
of our family taken over the past twenty years in the various
rooms of the house and surrounding grounds.
AT RISE: Light slowly bleeds through the scrim revealing the living
room and landing of the set. The furniture is still in place and
the charm of the room is only partially dissipated by a general
look of disarray and a number of cardboard packing cases that
litter the rugs and pegged floors. The scrim disappears as BAR-
BARA HARTMAN, an attractive, feminine woman in her for-

*ties, wearing jeans and a shirt and carrying a packing case filled
with odds and ends, comes down the stairs, deposits the case,
looks around the room, and becomes overwhelmed with nostal-
gia. She moves about aimlessly, sometimes pausing to touch cer-
tain objects that are obviously triggering specific memories.
Behind her we see MILDRED, a large, handsome, ageless black
woman appear in the kitchen doorway. She stands, a mug of
coffee in her hand, observing BARBARA.)*

MILDRED. How you feeling?
BARBARA. Shaky.

(MILDRED moves to her with coffee.)

MILDRED. Here, sit down and drink this while you can. Pretty
soon all hell's going to break loose.

*(BARBARA sits with coffee as MILDRED moves to window to open
drapes and let in the weak October sunlight.)*

BARBARA. I've never moved before. Is it that bad?
MILDRED. Well, it ain't no day at the beach.
BARBARA. *(Troubled.)* You think I'm doing the right thing,
Mildred? *(Mildred turns to look at her.)* Dumb question, huh?
MILDRED. World keeps spinning around.
BARBARA. You sure you're going to be all right, Mildred?
MILDRED. Oh, I'll be just fine.
BARBARA. You going to retire?
MILDRED. At my age? No, I'll be moving on to something
else. A new challenge.
BARBARA. No more domestic work?
MILDRED. Uh uh. I figure I got that down cold. I was thinking

of something more on the executive level. *(She moves to take BARBARA's mug.)* Now you stop worrying about me.

BARBARA. I've never had to worry about you, have I? In twenty-five years I can't remember you coming to me with one problem.

MILDRED. *(Lightly.)* Oh, my problems are much too lurid for this neighborhood, Mrs. Hartman. *(A beat— seriously.)* It was nice to know I always could though. *(A moment of contact.)* I'd better get breakfast started.

(She moves toward the kitchen.)

BARBARA. Mildred? *(She turns.)* Do you know what I'm going to miss most? Your company.

MILDRED. Mrs. Hartman, you are the nicest woman.

(MILDRED EXITS. BARBARA takes a breath and moves to finish the packing that MILDRED started as FRED SAPSTEAD, a physically spry man in his late seventies ENTERS and moves to a table covered with various potted plants.)

FRED. Were you looking for me?

BARBARA. Matter of fact I was.

FRED. I was in Mildred's room.

BARBARA. What were you doing in there, Dad?

FRED. I was talking to her about my plants. I'm leaving her all my plants, you know.

BARBARA. I know, Dad.

FRED. All except this African violet. Best plant I ever had. Had it— what? — over two years and it never stops blooming. Just water it twice a week and it blooms. *(He holds it up.)* Just look at that beauty.

MOVING

BARBARA. It's lovely, Dad. *(She calls.)* Mildred!

(MILDRED pokes her head into the room.)

BARBARA. Could you fix some breakfast for Dad?
MILDRED. Sure thing. I'm fixing you some popovers, Fred.
FRED. Thank you, my dear.

(MILDRED EXITS. FRED gazes after her with admiration.)

FRED. You know, there are many things I admire about Mildred but her popovers rank high on my list.

(BARBARA goes back to packing.)

BARBARA. I don't know where she gets her energy. I've never been able to find out who old she is but she must be in her sixties, wouldn't you think?
FRED. Well, I don't know but she has the body of a fifty year old.
BARBARA. How do you know?
FRED. *(Matter-of-factly.)* I saw her in the shower.

(He goes back to tending his plants.)

BARBARA. When?
FRED. I don't know. Recently I think.
BARBARA. *(Slightly shocked.)* And you looked?
FRED. Of course. How many chances do I get to look at naked women anymore?
BARBARA. What did she say?
FRED. She said, "This is not a good time to discuss your plants,

Fred." *(Thinks.)* Right. So it must have been recently. Anyway, I could understand her position. She wasn't rude or anything— Mildred is never rude— so after a moment or two I discretely withdrew. *(He is looking out rear window.)* Why is there a body in the tree?

BARBARA. What?

FRED. *(Peering.)* Looks like a creature up at the top of the big maple. Funny, almost looks human.

(BARBARA has resumed packing and is not paying attention.)

BARBARA. Dad, are you wearing your glasses?

FRED. No, I must have put them down somewhere.

BARBARA. Well, you'd better find them while you can. The movers will be here any moment and it's going to be very confusing.

(He turns to face her.)

FRED. Yes, that's why I wanted to talk to you now before it's too late.

BARBARA. Too late for what?

FRED. The thing is— I've come to a decision, I don't think we should move to Albuquerque.

BARBARA. Dad, the movers are on their way! I don't have time to talk about this now!

(This hurts him but he covers it by getting angry and huffy.)

FRED. Well, if that's the way you feel about it, I may as well watch baseball.

MOVING

(He plumps himself down in front of a TV set. The screen is visible to us.)

BARBARA. *(Unbelieving.)* You're going to watch baseball in the living room while we're moving?

FRED. It may be my last season.

(He flicks on the set. There is no picture, just a low humming and a grainy black and white static. BARBARA tries to get control of herself.)

BARBARA Okay — okay— I'm sorry I snapped at you. We'll talk— but will you please make it brief?

(He turns to face her.)

FRED. All right. Why are we moving to that place?

BARBARA. I've told you the reasons. Don't you remember?

FRED. Don't treat me like an idiot, Barbara. Of course I do.

BARBARA. Then what are they?

FRED. Is this a test?

BARBARA. I'm not sure you were listening.

FRED. You have an old friend there who just got divorced. She's good at business and you're a wonderful cook so you're going to open a restaurant there. Do I pass?

BARBARA. I'm sorry.

FRED. There's something wrong with this picture. The players look fuzzy.

BARBARA. There is no picture, Dad. Mildred must have disconnected the aerial.

FRED. No, I just think it's taking longer to warm up.

BARBARA. *(Cracking.)* We're moving, Dad! The aerial's been

disconnected! *(She hits the off button.)* We're moving!!

    FRED. *(Bemused.)* Well, there's no need to get hysterical.

    BARBARA. Look, Dad, I really don't have any more time right now. *(Moving to stairs.)* I have to strip the bed linen off the beds before the movers — *(She has glanced out the window.)* Oh, my God, there's someone sitting in the maple tree!

    FRED. Told you so.

    BARBARA. *(Puzzled.)* It's Timmy. What's he doing up in the tree? *(She moves to French doors.)* He hasn't climbed that tree since he was nine. *(She opens French doors, calls.)* Timmy! Timmy, what are you doing up there?

(She EXITS to garden. Fred is oblivious to her departure and talks as Mildred, carrying a tray of breakfast enters from kitchen.)

    FRED. I just don't know how you can do this to your children.

(MILDRED sets up tray during following:)

    MILDRED. The children have gone, Fred. Hilary's in England and Jennifer's in college. Okay, maybe it'll be hard on Timmy but, Fred— in a couple of years he'll be off to college too.

    FRED. Why are you calling me Fred?

    MILDRED. I've always called you Fred.

(He sees who it is.)

    FRED. Oh, it's you, my dear. Might have known it wasn't Barbara. She never listens.

(BARBARA and TIMMY, a studious-looking, very bright boy of fifteen, ENTER.)

BARBARA. You mean you've been up there for two hours? I don't understand.

TIMMY. Neither do I really. Probably some primal urge to return to my childhood.

MILDRED. I'll get you some breakfast.

(She EXITS. BARBARA heads for stairs.)

BARBARA. I really have to strip those bed.

FRED. The children still have to have a place to come home to, you know.

BARBARA. They'll have a place to come home to, Dad.

FRED. Some condom in the middle of the desert.

BARBARA. That's condo, Dad. Condo!

(She moves up stairs. He calls after her.)

FRED. Yes, I know those places. If the walls could talk they'd have nothing to say!

(He moves back to his plants.)

TIMMY. Granddad, I — I need to get your advice about something.

FRED. What you want to talk about?

TIMMY. Sex.

FRED. Sex — that rings a bell somewhere. Give me a moment — it'll come back to me.

TIMMY. Stop kidding around, Granddad. This is serious.

FRED. Okay, but do you mind if we eat and watch baseball while we talk? *(He moves to turn set on, sits in front of it with break-*

fast tray.) At my age time gets short so I like to try to always do three things at once. *(There is still no TV picture.)* It takes a while to warm up. Fire away. *(Timmy sits opposite him.)*

TIMMY. Granddad, when did you lose your virginity?

FRED. *(Promptly.)* January 3rd, 1917. Four-thirty in the afternoon. Girl was a redhead. Cherie. French.

TIMMY. *(Amazed.)* You remember it that exactly?

FRED. Oh, yes.

TIMMY. That's amazing.

FRED. Yes, isn't it? It was a whorehouse.

TIMMY. What was?

FRED. My first time. Not the best initiation into the wonders of sensuality — but things were different then. What was your question?

TIMMY. *(Earnestly.)* Okay. If a person is really desperate to lose his virginity and he knows a nice girl he likes— really likes— is it fair to use an emotionally charged situation to take advantage of this girl?

FRED. Absolutely. *(A beat.)* Of course that's just me talking and I'm pretty desperate myself in that area.

(BARBARA comes down the stairs carrying a carton.)

BARBARA. I think I hear the moving van.

FRED. The point is, Barbara, just because you've had a spat with your husband is no reason to move to Albuquerque.

BARBARA. *(Sorely tried.)* Spat? Dad, Charlie left me over a year ago. We're divorced. He's living with another woman.

FRED. I hear she's gone bald.

BARBARA. *(Distracted.)* Who?

FRED. Charlie's tart.

BARBARA. She has a name, Dad. It's Valerie.

MOVING

FRED. Anyway, she's gone totally bald.
BARBARA. What?

(The doorbell rings.)

FRED. Charlie's tart. Bald as a badger.

(BARBARA moves to the front door still looking over her shoulder at her father and trying to absorb the information. She opens the door to reveal HARRY PICARDO, a very large, overweight, perspiring, panting man in his late fifties. We have caught him at a time in his life when, for reasons that will become apparent later, his behavior is extremely erratic and often borders on the truly bizarre. BARBARA looks at this heavy-breathing hulk of a man with some consternation.)

HARRY. *(Panting.)* Harry — Picardo — movers.
BARBARA. Is something the matter?
HARRY. Jesus — those stairs are killers.
BARBARA. *(Not understanding.)* There are only six of them.
HARRY. Yeah, but for a man my age. *(Lumbers into the room.)*
You got some place I can sit for a minute?
BARBARA. Uh — of course — over here.

(He sinks into a chair, still panting.)

BARBARA. Are you all right?
HARRY. My heart's palpitating. It's probably the anxiety.
BARBARA. Anxiety?
HARRY. Yeah, I'm always nervous that we won't find the house.
(He puts his hand on his wrist pulse.) Yeah, there she goes. Look, it may not mean a thing, but when you're my build you gotta watch it.

MOVING

Do you have a glass of water or something?

(BARBARA, TIMMY and FRED have been staring at him, absolutely transfixed.)

BARBARA. Uh — of course. Timmy, could you get — Mr. Picardo? *(He nods.)* A glass of water?

(TIMMY EXITS to the kitchen on the run.)

HARRY. Thanks— I'll be okay in a minute. Just let me get my wind back and we'll start in. Is my color okay? *(As TIMMY reenters with water.)* Thanks, kid. My son Joey's backing the truck up the driveway right now.
TIMMY. I'm going to watch.

(He exits through front door.)

HARRY. Yeah, well he's got more guts than me.
BARBARA. Guts?
HARRY. It's a big rig. I can't stand to watch. Not at my age.
BARBARA. *(Apprehensively.)* Uh — Mr. Picardo — how many of you are there?
HARRY. Just Joey and me.
BARBARA. *(Appalled.)* Just the two of you?
HARRY. And Bruno — if he sobers up.
BARBARA. *(Dully.)* Sobers up?
HARRY. He usually does — so I'd say we can almost definitely count on him. I thought he'd of slept it off by now but he still needs a coupla hours.
BARBARA. Mr. Picardo, this is a very big house. I don't think three men will be enough to manage it.

MOVING

HARRY. Look, lady, don't give me a hard time. I've had a lousy day.

BARBARA. *(Nonplussed.)* It's only seven o'clock in the morning.

HARRY. You think I got an easy life? What do you know about my life?

BARBARA. I'm sorry. I just mean —

(HARRY suddenly leaps to his feet.)

HARRY. Look, I don't need this! I mean I can't deal with this! *(His yelling has brought MILDRED in.)* Listen, I don't need this abuse this early in the morning! Just save it for later when it's more appropriate, okay?

FRED. When is that?

HARRY. About three, four in the afternoon. If you'd have given me a chance to make my speech you'd of known that!

MILDRED. What speech?

HARRY. It's not the right time yet! *(He regains control of himself, turns to a traumatized BARBARA.)* Look, I'm sorry I flew off the handle at you. You seem like a nice lady. It's just that lately I've— I've been off my feed and it's made me a bit— grouchy, you know?

BARBARA. I'm sorry but you see we have a lot of heavy furniture. We have a piano on the second floor that—

HARRY. A piano? You're worried about a piano?

(She manages to nod.)

HARRY. You're talking to me about pianos? You want to know about pianos? I never lost a piano in my life! *(Feels his heart.)* Beating fast. Whew! I need to take a break.

MOVING

BARBARA. Mr. Picardo, you're making me very nervous. With just the three of you —

HARRY. Listen, we'll be okay. So just relax and let us take care of everything, okay?

(BARBARA manages a nod. There is a sickening crash of wood being splintered outside and the house shakes with the impact. There is a moment's horrified silence. HARRY, still sitting, speaks in a very controlled voice.)

HARRY. I— really— hate it when he does that.

BARBARA. What— what happened?

(TIMMY ENTERS on the run.)

TIMMY. The moving truck backed into the carport roof! There's wood all over the driveway!

BARBARA. Oh, my God!

(She and TIMMY EXIT. Mildred follows at a more leisurely pace. HARRY remains seated.)

FRED Do you like plants?

(HARRY just stares at him.)

FRED. *(Continued.)* I have this African violet. Blooms all the time. Just water it twice a week and it blooms.

HARRY. No shit.

(JOEY PICARDO, a lithe young man in his early twenties, ENTERS. HARRY gets to his feet.)

JOEY. It's probably not as bad as it sounded.

HARRY. *(Advancing toward him.)* Why did you back into the carport? Didn't you look where you were going?

JOEY. That's a stupid question.

(HARRY punches JOEY's shoulder on every word, increasing the force each time.)

HARRY. What about backing into the carport. You — don't — think —that's — not — stupid!!

JOEY. Keep your hands to yourself or I'll deck you!

HARRY. *(Still punching.)* Oh yeah, that'll be the day!

(JOEY grabs him and the two start to wrestle.)

JOEY. You're acting like a crazy man, you know that!

HARRY. *(Still trying to pummel him.)* Keep your goddamn hands off me!

(They continue to wrestle around the room grunting and yelling. BARBARA, followed by TIMMY, ENTERS. They stop and stare at the spectacle.)

JOEY. I'm gonna break your arm if you don't quit!

HARRY. Yeah— and I'll smash your face in!

(JOEY notices that BARBARA and TIMMY have reentered, manages to wrap his arms around his father, pinning him into submission.)

JOEY He'll be okay, lady. He's — a bit overexcited. *(To*

HARRY.) You okay now, Pop?
    HARRY Just — just leave me alone.

(He breaks loose, sits, trying to get his breath.)

    JOEY. *(To BARBARA.)* I'm sorry about the carport. I think there's something wrong with the clutch. See, Bruno usually drives but I don't trust him when he's having marital problems.

(BARBARA makes a valiant attempt to regain her composure.)

    BARBARA. Uh — look, could we please get started?
    HARRY. Sure — no problem. *(To JOEY.)* Just check upstairs and see what we got on our hands here.
    JOEY. Right.

(He moves towards the stairs but in the middle of the room he suddenly leaps into the air in an extravagant balletic twirl. Everyone except HARRY is transfixed. JOEY bounds up the stairs and EXITS. Heads turn in unison back to HARRY.)

    HARRY. *(Balefully.)* He started dancing when his mother died.
    TIMMY. He didn't like her?
    HARRY. What are you talking — she was his mother.
    TIMMY. So you think it was some kind of psychological reaction?
    HARRY. I dunno. All I know is he just started dancing. Worries the hell out of me. He does it in the street, you know.
    BARBARA. Does what?
    HARRY. Leaping — twirls. I've watched him from the window. He'll be walking down the street alone and then suddenly he does it. The first time I yelled out "What the hell you think you're

doing?" He says "A pilé." You think that's easy? Having a kid who goes around pliéing right in the neighborhood?

(She doesn't know what to say.)

    HARRY. *(Continued.)* Kids — right?

(She shrugs. He struggles to his feet.)

    HARRY. *(Continued.)* Well, I'd better take a crack at them stairs.

(He lumbers towards the stairs. FRED goes back to his plants, BARBARA is about to resume packing when HARRY stops, turns.)

    HARRY. Oh, I forget to make my speech.
    BARBARA. What?
    HARRY. I always make a speech.

(FRED turns and the three stare up at HARRY.)

    HARRY. Okay, let's not kid around. Moving is not Christmas. Everyone is tense, nerves are raw, tempers are short. It's a traumatic event. Studies show that it ranks right up there with divorce, getting fired, and losing a loved one. On a more philosophical level, people are dealing with an overwhelming, bittersweet nostalgia and facing some uneasy tomorrows. People who are moving do not act in a normal fashion. I understand this but if we all pull together and keep our heads we can turn this into a productive experience. So — good luck and God bless.

(He EXITS up the stairs. Nobody moves for a moment.)

MOVING

FRED. *(Finally.)* It's an omen.

BARBARA. An omen?

FRED. We shouldn't move. God sent us a fruitcake so we wouldn't move.

BARBARA. Dad, that's not an omen.

FRED. And I suppose you don't think Charlie's tart going bald is an omen either?

BARBARA. What? Dad, you're exaggerating.

FRED. No, I'm not. She had to have this cyst cut off her head.

(HARRY and JOEY appear on landing carrying a dresser between them. They exchange the usual moving men dialogue: "From me," "To you," "Lift your end," etc., through following.)

FRED. *(Continued.)* They had to shave her head close as a billiard ball. *(To HARRY and JOEY.)* Talking about her husband's tart.

BARBARA. *(Embarrassed.)* Dad, this is no time to be discussing this!

FRED. I'm just trying to point out that you'd stand a much better chance now. *(To JOEY and HARRY.)* You'd better put that down. We're not sure we're moving yet.

(The two men look over at BARBARA.)

BARBARA. No, don't listen to him! Keep — keep going.

(JOEY and HARRY EXIT with dresser.)

FRED. Look, I never thought she was that hot to begin with but now she's a disaster.

MOVING

(BARBARA tries to remain calm.)

BARBARA. Mildred, would you finish the packing in the kitchen?

(MILDRED gives an understanding nod and EXITS.)

BARBARA. Timmy, go and make sure your toys are packed properly.

(TIMMY EXITS. BARBARA turns to FRED.)

BARBARA. Dad, would you please not discuss this in front of people while we're moving!

FRED. Barbara, every man has a few tarts in his life. Even me. I had one in Des Moines.

BARBARA. *(Moving away.)* I don't think I want to hear about this.

(HARRY and JOEY reenter and trudge through room.)

JOEY. Bruno's looking better.

BARBARA. What? Oh, good.

(HARRY and JOEY move upstairs but are obviously interested in the conversation and listen until they EXIT.)

FRED. Anyway, your mother got wind of it. Never said a word but I could tell. But she didn't just roll over and give up like you did. No sir, when I drove to Omaha she made sure she came with me.

(BARBARA, puzzled, looks up from packing.)

MOVING

BARBARA. Why?

FRED. Because that's where my tart was. I was a salesman on the road. Haven't you been listening?

BARBARA. Wasn't your girlfriend in Des Moines?

FRED. Probably. Those two places look very similar. Anyway, I do remember it was a blue and white DeSoto.

BARBARA. What was?

FRED. The car we drove in. That put an end to it.

BARBARA. Dad, it wasn't the same thing as with Charlie. He went through a whole life change!

(HARRY and JOEY reappear with another item of furniture.)

FRED. What's different? I almost moved to Des Moines!

(She gives an exasperated sigh, moves away. He follows her.)

FRED. *(Continued.)* Look, Barbara, my advice is to strike while the iron is hot before her hair grows back in.

(BARBARA finally loses control.)

BARBARA. Dad, the problem with our marriage had nothing to do with Valerie!

FRED. *(Blankly.)* Who's Valerie?

BARBARA. Charlie's tart!!

FRED. Does this mean that you're definitely moving them?

(HARRY and JOEY stop in their tracks, wait for her answer.)

BARBARA. Of course it does.

FRED. Well, in that case I think you should know I'm not coming. *(He heads for the kitchen.)* Just don't count on me for Albuquerque.

BARBARA. Dad —

(But he has EXITED. BARBARA turns to see HARRY and JOEY waiting.)

BARBARA. *(Continued.)* Yes?

HARRY. Who should we listen to?

BARBARA. Me! Listen to me! He!

(They shrug and are about to make for door when JENNIFER HARTMAN, a tomboyish, energetic, athletic girl in her early twenties, ENTERS. She is absolutely loaded down with knapsacks, suitcases, etc.)

JENNIFER. *(Cheerfully.)* Hey, which bozo backed the rig into the carport?

BARBARA. *(Very surprised.)* Jennifer, what are you doing here?

JENNIFER. I got homesick. So who was the bozo who trashed the garage?

JOEY. This bozo.

JENNIFER. New on the job?

JOEY. You think backing up a two-ton rig is easy?

(JENNIFER starts to unload her stuff.)

JENNIFER. Nope. Took me about half an hour before I'd mastered it. That was when I was thirteen.

JOEY. *(To BARBARA.)* Is she kidding?

BARBARA. No, she's very mechanical. Look, could you please

keep moving?

(JOEY and HARRY EXIT with furniture. JENNIFER is strewing her stuff on floor.)

BARBARA. *(Continued.)* Jennifer, we're trying to take stuff out of here not bring it in. Now what are you doing here?

JENNIFER. I was worried about Granddad. I think he may be going loony.

BARBARA. Why?

JENNIFER. Well, you know how he writes me about twice a week. Well, lately he's been writing these messages on the outside of the envelopes.

BARBARA. What kind of messages?

(JENNIFER is sorting through mail.)

JENNIFER. Well, for instance, a couple of weeks ago he wrote on the outside of this envelope "Turned out he had to lose the leg." Naturally it scared the hell out of me. I ripped open the envelope and found out he was talking about the Sloans' cocker spaniel.

BARBARA. Well, he's always been close to that dog.

JENNIFER. Mum, you don't understand. There were other messages like "Don't tell your mother. It's not something I'm proud of."

BARBARA. What did that mean?

JENNIFER. I can't tell you but it involved triplets. *(As Barbara blanches.)* Don't worry — it was some time ago. Then yesterday I got this. *(She hands her a crumpled envelope.)* Read the outside.

BARBARA. *(Reading.)* "Your father's tart has gone totally bald."

JENNIFER. Now do you see what I mean?

BARBARA. Well, actually she has. Evidently she had this cyst on her—

JENNIFER. Mum, that's not the point! You don't go around writing that sort of thing on the outside of envelopes unless you're not dealing from a full deck. Is he okay?

BARBARA. Yes, he's fine. He's just getting a little vague, that's all.

JENNIFER. Well, I wanted to make sure.

(BARBARA looks at her for a moment.)

BARBARA. Okay, Jennifer— now what's the real reason for your coming home?

JENNIFER. I quit college.

BARBARA. *(Appalled.)* What?

(At this point, FRED, carrying some crates to put his plants in, ENTERS.)

FRED. Did I hear Jenny's voice? Is that Jennifer?

JENNIFER. In person.

(She embraces her grandfather.)

FRED. You owe me a letter.

JENNIFER. How you doing, Granddad?

FRED. Packing my plants. I don't trust those two fruitcakes posing as moving men.

JENNIFER. Here, let me help.

(She takes some crates, packs some plants during the following:)

MOVING

BARBARA. Jennifer, what is going on here? What are your plans?

JENNIFER. I thought I'd work at some odd jobs — maybe as an aerobics instructor — until I piled up enough money.

BARBARA. Enough money for what?

(JENNIFER turns to face her.)

JENNIFER. To open up a garage.

(HARRY, puffing, and JOEY ENTERS. BARBARA is staring at JENNIFER.)

JENNIFER. Just a small place. Maybe specialize in foreign cars.

BARBARA. I think I'm going crazy.

HARRY. Something the matter, Mrs. Hartman?

BARBARA. My daughter has just told me she wants to become a garage mechanic.

HARRY. Whatever happened to girls wanting to be nurses and boys wanting to be firemen?

JENNIFER. We're trying not to be restricted by gender any more.

HARRY. *(Becomes excited.)* Don't give me that crazy talk! All I hear is crazy talk!

JOEY. Take it easy, Pop. *(To JENNIFER.)* My father's very old-fashioned.

HARRY. Does it mean I'm old-fashioned just because I like everything the way it used to be? I don't like broads with grease under their fingernails or guys who smell nice, okay?

JOEY. Pop, calm down — you'll have a coronary.

HARRY. I won't have a "coronary!" If I have anything it'll be a good old-fashioned heart attack! Anyway, I'm in as good a shape as

I ever was! Now help me up those goddamn stairs!

(JOEY helps his Father upstairs. JENNIFER watches them EXIT, her attention on JOEY.)

JENNIFER. Cute ass.
FRED. *(Looking up from plants.)* Well, I try and keep in shape.
JENNIFER. Not you, Granddad.
BARBARA. Jennifer, exactly where do you plan on doing all this?
JENNIFER. Well, I was thinking of coming to Albuquerque to live with you.
BARBARA. *(Appalled.)* Jennifer, there's no room in Albuquerque.
FRED. She can have my room. *(As BARBARA looks at him.)* I told you I'm not going.

(JENNIFER is distracted by the sound of a piano playing the commercial jingle from upstairs.)

BARBARA. Don't be ridiculous, Dad. If you don't come with us where will you go?
FRED. Don't know yet. Maybe I'll just hit the open road.

(JENNIFER moves to the bottom of the stairs.)

BARBARA. There is no open road any more!
FRED. Just a figure of speech. I'll ride the rods.
JENNIFER. You didn't tell me Dad was here.
BARBARA. What?
JENNIFER. That's his jingle. Has he been here all day?
BARBARA. *(Very shaken.)* I — I don't know.

MOVING

JENNIFER. I'll bring him down. Dad!
BARBARA. Jennifer —

(But JENNIFER has EXITED.)

FRED. I told you he'd come back. Just in the nick of time.

(They EXIT. JENNIFER comes down the stairs with CHARLIE.)

JENNIFER. Look who I found!

(A moment of tension as CHARLIE and BARBARA look at one another.)

CHARLIE. *(Finally.)* You ever get the feeling we're drifting apart?
BARBARA. What are you doing here?
CHARLIE. I guess I wanted to say goodbye to the house.
BARBARA. Anyway I thought you said goodbye to the house a year ago.
CHARLIE. No. You and the kids were still here so I always felt— a connection.

(They are looking at one another as JOEY ENTERS on to the landing.)

JOEY. Anyone seen Bruno? Sometimes he wanders off to get an after breakfast brandy.
JENNIFER. Could you use another strong set of muscles?
JOEY. Sure. Know anybody?

(She makes a gesture, follows him up the stairs and they EXIT.)

MOVING

CHARLIE. Growing up.

BARBARA. But not maturing. Did she tell you she's quit school?

CHARLIE. Sure. We talk about twice a week.

BARBARA. Nobody accused you of being a bad father, Charlie.

CHARLIE. Going to be rough though with Timmy three thousand miles away.

BARBARA. I'm not moving to spite you.

(He hands her a vase which she packs.)

CHARLIE. I know. You're not perfect but you couldn't be petty if you tried.

BARBARA. Oh, I tried. I just couldn't get the hang of it.

(CHARLIE is looking up at beams on ceiling.)

BARBARA. *(Continued.)* I've been managing quite well on my own, Charlie. What is it?

CHARLIE. Oh, I was remembering when we stripped all the beams and doors. Remember when we bought the place it was all red and gold? We kept hitting new layers of paint. Yellow.

BARBARA. That was the Newleys.

CHARLIE. Green.

BARBARA. The Carltons.

CHARLIE. Silver.

BARBARA. The Templetons.

CHARLIE. Were we the first family who lived here who had taste?

BARBARA. We thought so.

CHARLIE. It took us six weeks and four bottles of liniment for our aching backs. It was like gold when we finally hit the natural woodwork.

(CHARLIE looks at BARBARA.)

    CHARLIE. *(Continued.)* That was our best time, wasn't it?
    BARBARA. Oh?
    CHARLIE. I'd just landed that big perfume account, we finally had some money, the kids were all pre-adolescent, pre-bad grades, pre-drugs, and we — we were —
    BARBARA. Still in love. You can say it.
    CHARLIE. The best of times, Barbara.

*(There is a moment of connection between them that is broken as
    JOEY and JENNIFER ENTER landing carrying a chest of draw-
    ers. BARBARA turns away, resumes packing.)*

    JENNIFER. I don't get it. If you want to dance why don't you study full time?
    JOEY. If I did the business would fall apart. I couldn't do that to Pop. It's all he's got.
    JENNIFER. Well, I think people should be able to do what they want. Lift your end — yeah, that's it. I like to fix cars. I mean what's the big deal? Doesn't make me any less feminine — whatever the hell that is.
    JOEY. I know what it is. And you're very feminine. I'm an expert.
    JENNIFER. *(Teasing.)* Because you're Italian?
    JOEY. Because I'm gay. Better tip it sideways.
    JENNIFER. You're gay?
    JOEY. Don't tell Pop. It'd kill him.

(They EXIT.)

CHARLIE. Looks like you could use some help. Would you like me to stick around and give you a hand?

BARBARA. I don't need you to do that, Charlie.

CHARLIE. No, but I do. I need the catharsis.

(She looks at him.)

CHARLIE. Look, we had some nice memories here. But they became— tarnished. My fault. I just thought we could salvage those memories.

BARBARA. *(Steadily.)* How do we do that, Charlie?

CHARLIE. Put the past to rest. Together. Okay?

BARBARA. *(Finally.)* I can handle it if you can.

CHARLIE. Thanks.

(He moves to stairs, halfway up, stops, pensively runs her hand over wooden bannister, sees her watching him, gives a little shrug, EXITS. BARBARA slowly sits. MILDRED ENTERS.

LIGHTS come up on the cluttered gazebo outside. TIMMY, wearing an Indian headdress, is sorting through the toys of his childhood! LISA, a bespectacled girl of sixteen, ENTERS and watches him.)

LISA. Your mother said I'd find you here.

(TIMMY turns to look at her, indicates toys.)

TIMMY. I didn't realize I'd lived this long.

(She moves into the room, puts on cowboy hat. He grins at her, resumes packing. He clears his throat.)

TIMMY. *(Continued.)* I'm sorry about last night.

LISA. I'm sorry for dozing off.

TIMMY. It was my fault. While you were laying there beside me I was trying to referee an argument.

LISA. Between who?

TIMMY. My intellect and my glands.

LISA. And your intellect won?

TIMMY. Yeah — but it was close.

LISA. I was rooting for your glands.

TIMMY. They didn't need any encouragement.

(He picks up a red fire engine.)

LISA. Anyway, when I woke up you'd gone.

TIMMY. I decided it just wasn't fair to you.

LISA. Having sex?

TIMMY. Not with me going away today and all. That sort of bonding can be very dangerous.

(She sits, regards him.)

LISA. You know, we're probably the only two people in our entire school who are still virgins. Why do you think that is?

TIMMY. *(Matter-of-factly.)* Because we're both misfits.

LISA. Even misfits think about sex.

TIMMY. Oh, I think about it.

LISA. With me?

TIMMY. Yes.

LISA. Exclusively.

TIMMY. I'm not that much of a misfit.

MOVING

(He has taken out a battered panda bear. He holds it up.)

LISA. Pancake. *(She holds out her hand, he passes it to her and she gazes fondly at it.)* How long have you been thinking about it—with me?

TIMMY. Ten years.

LISA. You found me sexy when I was five?

TIMMY. Probably. I don't know— I just liked you.

LISA. Why?

TIMMY. Because you made me laugh. You were real funny looking.

LISA. And why do you like me now?

TIMMY. Same reason.

(She hits him with the cowboy hat, his laugh fades as he looks into her eyes.)

LISA. I've been having some— interesting fantasies about you too, Timmy.

TIMMY. You have?

(They embrace and kiss feverishly.)

BARBARA. *(Offstage.)* Lisa, are you in there?

(They leap apart.)

TIMMY. Suddenly I feel about nine years old.

LISA. And playing doctor. *(Calling.)* What is it, Mrs. Hartman?

BARBARA. *(Offstage.)* Your mother phoned. Your parents just got home from the airport.

LISA. I'll be right there. *(She moves to the door, turns.)* Hold the thought. I'll be back as soon as I can.

TIMMY. They'll be coming into this room soon. Somebody's liable to walk in while we're doing it and crate us!

LISA. Look, we both have IQ's in the high percentile and also a very strong animal drive.

TIMMY. *(Puzzled.)* So?

LISA. So we'll find a place. *(A beat— shyly.)* I'm glad you like me.

(She quickly EXITS. TIMMY starts to frantically prepare the room, notices "Pancake," picks it up, looks at it.)

TIMMY. Goodbye, childhood.

(He clutches "Pancake" to his chest, sits. Lights slowly fade on gazebo and crossfade to living room. BARBARA looks up from packing as CHARLIE comes downstairs.)

CHARLIE. Curly, Moe and Larry are starting to lower the piano out the window. I can't watch.

BARBARA. I'm sure they know what they're doing.

CHARLIE. No, it's not that. Too many memories. *(A moment of contact.)* You decided to take it to Albuquerque with you?

BARBARA. *(Turning away.)* No, there's not enough room there. I'm donating it to the local YMCA.

CHARLIE. *(Shocked.)* You're giving our piano away?

BARBARA. It seemed the best solution.

CHARLIE. But that piano's almost a hundred years old. It came with the house.

(She looks at him.)

CHARLIE. *(Continued.)* I don't know — I always felt it belonged here.

BARBARA. Nothing belongs here, Charlie.

(She turns away. Through the window on the upstage wall we see the piano being lowered outside— an inch at a time. It is suspended there throughout following scenes until indicated. CHARLIE moves to window, stares up at it.)

CHARLIE. God, we had some good times around that, didn't we?

BARBARA. It's just a thing, Charlie. Don't romanticize it out of all proportions.

CHARLIE. You used to say being a romantic was one of my more appealing qualities.

BARBARA. I was wrong.

CHARLIE. Not so appealing anymore?

BARBARA. Oh, yes. But you never really were a romantic were you?

CHARLIE. Oh?

BARBARA. Well, you certainly managed to walk out of here without a backward glance.

CHARLIE. I was a little crazy, Barbara.

BARBARA. I drove you crazy?

CHARLIE. *(To BARBARA— sincerely.)* I'm sorry.

(She moves away.)

BARBARA. *(Overly casual.)* How is Valerie? Still bald? *(As he looks at her.)* Dad told me.

CHARLIE. She's probably fine.

BARBARA. Probably?

CHARLIE. We split up three weeks ago.

BARBARA. *(Finally.)* Why?

CHARLIE. Valeria wasn't the answer.

BARBARA. What is the answer, Charlie?

CHARLIE. I don't know. I'm just beginning to ask the questions— honestly. Do you think you can ever forgive me?

(We see her attitude towards him soften.)

BARBARA. *(Finally.)* I'm sorry about the piano, Charlie. I had no other choice.

(They are looking at one another as JENNIFER and MAVIS CRUIKSHANK, a middle-aged, blowsily overdressed, rather ditsy, real estate woman, carrying a bag and a briefcase, EN-TER.)

JENNIFER. Mom, someone to see you.

(JENNIFER crosses to continue packing FRED's plants as BARBARA introduces MAVIS to CHARLIE and then sits as MA-VIS extracts a sheaf of escrow papers.)

MAVIS. Okay, all we need is your John Hancock— here— here— and here— and let's see— initial where the exxes are.

(As BARBARA is looking over forms MAVIS glances over at CHARLIE, who has been watching without any enjoyment.)

MAVIS. *(Continued.)* Listen, I'll tell you the truth — I was never sure this day would come. I mean white elephants like this are hard to move in today's market. See, it has a lot of wood.

MOVING

CHARLIE. *(Nonplussed.)* Yes, it does have wood.

MAVIS. People don't want wood. Today, they want contemporary. New materials that don't need upkeep. *(To BARBARA.)* Don't forget to initial the changes. They want plumbing.

CHARLIE. We have plumbing.

MAVIS. Plumbing that works— in modern colors. Well, what with the high interest rates and all I knew I had one tough sale on my hands. But I persevered — got creative. That's what real estate is all about— perseverance and creativity.

CHARLIE. Yes— well, I hope the family that moves in will be as happy as we were.

MAVIS. Family? We're not selling to a family.

BARBARA. *(Quickly.)* Do I sign here too?

MAVIS. That's right, dearie. *(To CHARLIE.)* Didn't Mrs. Hartman tell you? We sold it to a real estate developer?

CHARLIE. *(Puzzled.)* Why would a real estate developer be interested in this house?

MAVIS. Oh, he doesn't want the house. It's the land he's interested in.

BARBARA. Mavis—

MAVIS. He's going to tear down the house and put up condominiums.

CHARLIE. My God, you sold our home to a developer?

(MILDRED ENTERS from the kitchen.)

MILDRED. What's the matter?

JENNIFER. Mom sold our house to someone who's going to tear it down!

MILDRED. No, I don't believe it.

BARBARA. I had no choice! I had to!

MOVING

(JENNIFER, CHARLIE, MILDRED, MAVIS all start yelling at once with BARBARA trying to answer.)

BARBARA. Will everyone stop screaming and listen to me!! *(This has some effect.)* You think I wanted the house to be torn down? You heard— it's a depressed market. The house was up for sale for over a year and we didn't even get a nibble.

MAVIS. She's right — not even a nibble. People today want modern.

BARBARA. What was I supposed to do?

MAVIS. They want formica, they want synthetics.

BARBARA. Sit here for the rest of my life like— like Miss Haversham and watch the place decay around me?

MAVIS. Right. People don't want old fashioned. They think old fashioned it out of date! They want bidets, they want—

CHARLIE. *(Cutting in.)* Mildred, Jennifer— everyone— will you please leave Barbara and I alone for a few moments. Please?

(JENNIFER, holding FRED'S African violet, EXITS upstairs. MILDRED EXITS to kitchen. MAVIS doesn't move.)

CHARLIE. *(Continued.)* Uh — Mavis — Barbara and I need some privacy.

MAVIS. Wouldn't you like to finish signing the closing papers first?

(He takes her arm, ushers her towards the door.)

CHARLIE. She can sign them later — if she wants.

MAVIS. Okay, but deals can fall apart at the last minute, you know and —

(He closes door on her, turns to face BARBARA.)

BARBARA. Don't look at me if I just drew a mustache on the Mona Lisa. I love this house as much as you do. Maybe more.

CHARLIE. Then why?

BARBARA. Because I had to get on with my life. Don't you understand? I had no life left here and my future was fast running out. I need a future.

CHARLIE. Even if it means destroying our past?

BARBARA. Look, it's my house and —

CHARLIE. Legally, that's all! I have an emotional stake here!

BARBARA. You want to buy the house? *(She waves forms at him.)* I'll sell it to you at the same price.

CHARLIE. You know I don't have that sort of money.

BARBARA. Do you have another solution, Charlie? Because if you do I'd really like to hear it.

(At this point a very distraught JENNIFER, holding her Grandfather's African violet, rushes onto the landing. Note: from this moment on the events leading up to the curtain happen in rapid succession, one catastrophe piling upon the other almost without a beat.)

BARBARA. Jennifer, what is it?

JENNIFER. I've — I've just found out something— terrible!

(She holds out the plant in front of her.)

CHARLIE. What's that?

JENNIFER. *(Almost incoherent.)* It's Granddad's African violet he — always talks about. Says — says it's the best plant he ever had. Waters it twice a week and it — it blooms all the time and — and —

CHARLIE. Calm down, honey. What is it?

JENNIFER. *(Wailing.)* It's plastic!
CHARLIE. What?
JENNIFER. The plant is plastic.
CHARLIE. *(Mystified.)* So what?
JENNIFER. My God, don't you understand?
CHARLIE. No. *(To BARBARA.)* Do you?

(BARBARA slowly sits.)

BARBARA. *(Quietly.)* It means he's — he's senile, Charlie.
CHARLIE. Oh, my God.

(There is an anguished yell from upstairs and the piano outside crashes to the ground outside the window with an absolutely horrendous noise of breaking wood and twanging piano wires. MILDRED enters from the kitchen as CHARLIE, BARBARA and JENNIFER rush to the window. TIMMY and LISA, half clothed, rush in.)

LISA. What — what is it?
TIMMY. They dropped the piano.
LISA. *(Relieved.)* I thought it was Godi

(LISA and TIMMY start to scramble into their clothes as HARRY Picardo, a comatose look on his face, appears on the landing. BARBARA, MILDRED, CHARLIE and JENNIFER turn to look at him.)

HARRY. *(Catatonic.)* I just lost the piano. I never lost a piano in my life. *(He slowly descends the stairs and proceeds to have a nervous breakdown.)* Bureaus I have — chandeliers — highboys — never lost — armoires — Rodins — brandy — piano — never lost a piano

MOVING

(He sinks onto the stairs. MILDRED and CHARLIE move to comfort him.)

HARRY. *(Continued.)*— toys and cameras— biedermere— uprights, grands— never lost— never harmed a spinet— never lost—

(He starts to cry loud, racking sobs.)

TIMMY. What's the matter with Mr. Picardo?
BARBARA. *(On the brink herself— dead voice.)* Our mover is having a nervous breakdown.

(The front door bursts open and a GIRL in punk clothes and a wild, bright, purple and orange hair-do enters with bags.)

HILARY. Hi Mom— hi Dad.

(CHARLIE and BARBARA peer at her.)

CHARLIE. *(Unbelieving.)* Hilary— is that you? What are you doing in America?

(She opens her coat to reveal she is very pregnant.)

HILARY. I wanted to have my baby at home, *(She looks around.)* Hey, what's going on here?

(There is a clap of thunder and rain starts to pour down.)

CURTAIN

END OF ACT ONE

ACT II

(It is one hour later.

AT RISE: BARBARA is sitting up a tree outside the house, gloomily contemplating the events of the day. JOEY comes out of the house, does one or two stretches before he notices BARBARA.)

JOEY. What are you doing up there, Mrs. Hartman?

BARBARA. Running away from home.

JOEY. How's it going?

BARBARA. How's it going? My chief moving man, having had a nervous breakdown, is lying in the attic like a beached whale, heavily sedated by two pills of unknown chemical substance, administered by my daughter— the one with the purple and orange hair— who has returned home, quite enceinte and extremely unmarried with the untimely statement that she wants to have the baby and raise it in the family home.

JOEY. What's enceinte?

BARBARA. Pregnant. My other daughter, Jennifer, the college dropout, ever the optimist is trying to repair the broken down moving van while she makes plans to work pumping gas. My ex-husband Charlie, a man of sudden exits and entrances is trying to resolve some inner conflict of his own, while our son Timmy, is trying to grab the reins of his galloping hormones. Have I remembered everyone? Oh no, my father, I have just discovered is fighting a losing battle with time. The good news— it's stopped raining. But

43

thanks for asking.

(He holds up his hand and she climbs down. The LIGHTS CROSSFADE to the other side of the house where JENNIFER is working on engine parts that are spread over the lawn. HILARY approaches, stops, regards the mess.)

HILARY. You sure you know how to put all that back together?

JENNIFER. Nope.

HILARY. *(With some admiration.)* Yeah, you always did just — plunge in.

JENNIFER. Look who's talking.

HILARY. You have grease on your nose.

JENNIFER. Thanks. And would you like to explain your appearance.

HILARY. Oh, it's just a passing phase. As a matter of fact, I'm thinking of washing it out.

JENNIFER. I don't mean your hair. Hilary. I mean your life.

HILARY. No, you don't. You mean my pregnancy.

(JENNIFER looks at her.)

JENNIFER. So what happened?

HILARY. Oh, I just got sick of being good.

JENNIFER. That doesn't make sense.

HILARY. Maybe not to you. You could always try anything you wanted and get away with it.

JENNIFER. You couldn't.

HILARY. I was the good one.

JENNIFER. You didn't have to be. You were the first born. All the other roles were still open.

HILARY. I made a bad choice. Blame it on my youth. You want

to hear a resume of my life?

    JENNIFER. Hil, I know about your life. I'm your sister.

    HILARY. But we were never that close, were we?

(JENNIFER looks at her, surprised by the admission.)

    JENNIFER. *(Finally.)* No. Why was that?

    HILARY Not easy having a tightass older sister who leaves a trail of straight A's wherever she goes.

(JENNIFER shrugs.)

    HILARY. *(Continued.)* Did you know I was toilet trained when I was ten months?

    JENNIFER. Yeah, there's a plague in the bathroom. Look, Hil, could we get to the Fall from Grace part?

    HILARY. I was working late one night in the library and — my don was there.

    JENNIFER. The father is an Oxford Don?

    HILARY. No, the janitor. His name is Don.

(A moment as JENNIFER absorbs this.)

    JENNIFER. But he was your type.

    HILARY. Jen, the pathetic part was I didn't even have a type.

    JENNIFER. Hil, help me out here. I'm trying to find something to recommend him.

    HILARY. He fancied me.

    JENNIFER. Well, that's something.

    HILARY. He fancied everybody.

    JENNIFER. And he was available.

    HILARY. Sort of. When he could get away from his wife and

kids.

JENNIFER. But you went to bed with him anyway?

HILARY. Not bed exactly. He offered to drive me home from the library.

JENNIFER. You did it in his car?

HILARY. No, he had a motor bike.

JENNIFER. Are you telling me you conceived in/on a motor bike?

HILARY. A side car. That's one of those passenger gismos they attach to a motor bike.

JENNIFER. So he parked the side car.

HILARY. No, he crashed it.

JENNIFER. Crashed it?

HILARY. Into a ditch.

JENNIFER. And that's where it happened? In a crashed side car in a ditch of some country road outside Oxford?

HILARY. No. In Oxford. The High Street. It was very embarrassing.

JENNIFER Yeah, well we all do embarrassing things when we're breathing heavily.

HILARY. No, I don't mean that. Turned out he'd stolen it.

JENNIFER. He was a thief?

HILARY. Yes, but only petty. And very unsuccessful. I didn't know this and called for the police to pull us out of the ditch. While we were waiting— sex reared its ugly head.

JENNIFER. Sounds so Victorian.

HILARY. But in this case very apt.

JENNIFER. But you kept seeing him?

HILARY. Only until he went to prison.

JENNIFER. Why?

HILARY. It didn't have anything to do with him, Jen. It was me.

MOVING

(JENNIFER beams at her.)

HILARY. Why are you looking so happy?
JENNIFER. Because I'm so glad you finally screwed up!!

(JENNIFER embraces her, breaks, pats HILARY's stomach.)

JENNIFER. Why did you decide to keep the baby?
HILARY. Sometimes bright people can be very lonely.
JENNIFER. And you really wanted to raise him here?
HILARY. All appearances to the contrary— I had a lovely childhood.

(The two women embrace and as the lights fade on them and crossfade to BARBARA in the house who is aimlessly moving around the room, packing odds and ends without apparent purpose. CHARLIE, carrying a plate of brownies, ENTERS.)

CHARLIE. *(Surprised.)* You're still packing?
BARBARA. *(A slight shrug.)* I don't know what else to do. You know me — when in doubt find an activity. And right now I'm "in doubt."
CHARLIE. There's only one solution, Barbara. A double suicide pact. *(He holds up plate.)* We'll OD on Mildred's brownies.
BARBARA. Still using jokes to shut out reality, Charlie?
CHARLIE. What do you expect? I have a daughter — the good one with two PhD.'s — who just showed up looking like trick or treat and seven months pregnant.
BARBARA. Eight months. She lied to the airline.
CHARLIE. Hilary lied?
BARBARA. Have you talked to her about it?

CHARLIE. No. Oh, we hugged and kissed a lot but as you know I try to avoid all emotional confrontations unless they're heavily underscored with a string section.

BARBARA. I remember.

CHARLIE. *(Suddenly.)* What happened to us, kid?

BARBARA. Think hard and it'll come back to you.

CHARLIE. I don't mean Valerie. What happened to us?

(She turns away with a small shrug.)

BARBARA. Wear and tear. Maybe we only had twenty-five years in us.

CHARLIE. Then why the hell do I miss you so much?

(She turns to look at him.)

BARBARA. When did you decide that?

CHARLIE. Soon after we split up. I just didn't have the guts to admit it.

BARBARA. *(Steadily.)* I wish you had.

CHARLIE. I'm sorry. I know I caused you a lot of pain.

BARBARA. *(Wryly.)* Well, yes, I did go through a period when I thought every Country Western song was written specifically about me.

CHARLIE. Well, I wasn't exactly the Student Prince at Heidelberg either.

BARBARA. Why didn't you tell me before?

CHARLIE. Ah, there was a good reason for that. *(A beat.)* Stupidity. *(A beat— sincerely.)* I'm just not complete without you, Barbara.

BARBARA. *(Finally.)* Is this — a proposal?

CHARLIE. Yes. Twice in a lifetime offer. You just can't let them tear this house down, Barbara.

BARBARA. You love it that much?

CHARLIE. Yes, I love it that much. I love you that much. Look, I know what you're thinking. But it would be different this time.

BARBARA. In what way, Charlie?

CHARLIE. I'm not crazy anymore.

BARBARA. Oh?

CHARLIE. Don't you see, I got it all out of my system — my mid-life crisis— my search to "find myself."

BARBARA. Did you find out who that was, Charlie?

CHARLIE. Well, it wasn't Beethoven. *(With some difficulty.)* I found a guy who can write catchy commercial jingles but who is never going to produce anything great. A flawed, ordinary husband who makes mistakes but discovered his home and family are really what he values most in life. *(A beat.)* Do you think you could love a man like that?

BARBARA. *(Gently.)* Are you willing to settle for serenity, Charlie?

CHARLIE. Settle? I want to grab it with both hands. Will you marry me, Barbara?

BARBARA. *(Finally.)* I need a little time to — to decide.

CHARLIE. You don't have too much of that.

BARBARA. I know that. I just don't want to say "yes" or "no" for the wrong reasons. *(As he looks at her.)* The house, my father, the children. It has to be for us.

(He nods, gently kisses her, moves to the door, turns.)

CHARLIE. You all right?

BARBARA. It's been a funny kind of day.

CHARLIE. Funny peculiar or funny ha-ha?

BARBARA Funny, I didn't know it was going to turn out this

way.

(The lights crossfade to the gazebo outside the house where JOEY is using the railing to do some ballet exercises. JENNIFER, wiping her hands on a rag, moves to gazebo.)

JENNIFER. I fixed the truck. It was the distributor. I'd really like to take the whole engine apart and give it a major tune-up but at least it shouldn't give you any trouble for a few thousand miles.
JOEY. Wow, I'm impressed.

(He does a quick dancers leap.)

JENNIFER. Me too. You really got to do something about your dancing, Joey.
JOEY. That bad, huh?
JENNIFER. You're talented.
JOEY. Ah, what do you know.
JENNIFER. And neither will you unless you give it a real shot. Tell your father you have to study full time.
JOEY. It'll kill him.
JENNIFER. I doubt it.
JOEY. He'd kill me.
JENNIFER. Oh, so that's it, huh? No guts.
JOEY. Now you got it. I'll do it.
JENNIFER. When? When you going to do it?
JOEY. You're tough.
JENNIFER. Better believe it.

(The lights fade on them, and the lights come up on a small sofa in the garden. TIMMY and LISA, about to consummate their relationship. FRED ambles in. He is not wearing his glasses.)

MOVING

FRED. Ah, there you are. I've been looking all over for you. *(FRED moves to them, sits on the arm of the sofa. The two youngsters stare at him with unbelieving, round eyes.)* Look, I know you have a lot on your plate right now but there are a couple of things I'd like to get off my chest.

TIMMY. *(Finding his voice.)* Now?

FRED. You don't have to stop what you're doing — just listen to what I have to say. Barbara, it's about the business of the plants.

TIMMY. Granddad, Mom's not here.

FRED. What?

(TIMMY scrambles to his feet.)

FRED. *(Continued.)* Oh, it's you, Timmy. *(He peers at LISA.)* Ah— hello, Lisa. What are you doing here?

TIMMY. She's— uh— helping me pack my— toys.

(FRED looks at him for a moment but his face doesn't give anything away.)

FRED. Oh, well I was looking for your mother. *(He stands, moves to door.)* Sorry, I've been a bit — distracted. *(He turns at door.)* Oh, Timmy?

TIMMY. Yes, Granddad?

FRED. Zip up your fly.

(He EXITS into the house. The two look at one another.)

LISA. That— was— the most embarrassing experience of my life!

TIMMY. Yeah, if any more people walk in on us I'm liable to

do myself a permanent injury.

  LISA. Timmy, maybe someone's trying to tell us something.

(He points up with his fingers.)

  LISA. *(Continued.)* You mean — God?
  TIMMY. No. I mean there's one more place we can try!

(He takes her hand and they EXIT. The lights crossfade to BARBARA wrapping dishes in one of the crannies in the living room. There is a KNOCK at the door.)

  FRED. *(Offstage.)* It's me, Barbara.

(He ENTERS and she watches him with a mixture of curiosity and trepidation as he sits in a rocking chair beside her, looks at her for a moment.

  FRED. *(Continued. Finally— lightly.)* Life sure is funny, isn't it?
  BARBARA. *(Warily.)* Hysterical.
  FRED. Mildred told me you found out about the African violet, *(A slight beat— conversationally.)* It's amazing what they can do with plastic these days, isn't it?

(She is too stunned to answer.)

  FRED. *(Continued, seriously.)* I know how you feel, Barbara.
  BARBARA. *(Carefully.)* You do?
  FRED. Yep, it really knocked the pins out from under me too.
  BARBARA. I don't understand. You knew it was plastic?
  FRED. Not until yesterday— or was it the day before? Realized

MOVING

the damned thing had no scent. Felt like I'd been poleaxed. You see, I've known for some time I— I wasn't the man I used to be. *(A difficult, resigned shrug.)* But, there's a difference between knowing you're a quart short and realizing you're operating on an empty tank. *(Beat.)* Scared the bejesus out of me. Excuse my French, dear.

BARBARA *(Gently.)* Is that why you suddenly decided you couldn't move to Albuquerque with me, Dad?

FRED. *(Nods.)* Living here— surrounded by all the — the clues to my life I'd be able to muddle through for a while without being too much of a burden. But out there— I'd be a dead duck.

BARBARA. I'm sorry, Dad. I should have been more understanding.

FRED No, no, it's my fault. I should have been honest with you but— *(He stops.)* Well, here's the thing of it. I know I've never been a particularly— loving father. Not in my nature.

BARBARA Dad —

FRED Oh, I had — feelings but somehow I could never learn the knack of— how to show them.

(BARBARA's eyes are brimming. He frowns.)

FRED. *(Continued.)* Now this all ties in somehow but — oh yes, so I settled for always wanting you to think of me as a responsible father. I took pride in that. Too much perhaps.

(She reaches over and takes his hand. They smile affectionately at one another.)

BARBARA. *(Finally.)* Dad, I have a question.

FRED. Well, you're in luck. You've caught me in one of my more lucid moments.

BARBARA. When you made the discovery about the plant why

did you keep on bragging about it?

FRED. I was hoping you'd notice it wasn't the real McCoy. *(A beat.)* There are some things a father doesn't want to tell his daughter.

(They sit, holding hands, their eyes moist. MILDRED, carrying a tray with lunch for two, ENTERS, busies herself setting up a tray.)

MILDRED. I fed everybody who wants it in the kitchen but I managed to save enough for you two.

BARBARA. I don't think I can eat anything, Mildred.

MILDRED. You have to try, Mrs. Hartman. Can't make important decisions on an empty stomach. You two have a nice talk?

FRED. Yes, everything's just fine, my dear. I told Barbara everything.

(MILDRED straightens up.)

MILDRED. Oh, dear. I wish you'd spoken to me first, Fred. *(To BARBARA— awkwardly.)* It's— it's not what it seems, Mrs. Hartman.

(BARBARA is nonplussed.)

FRED. Mildred, I didn't tell her everything. Just about the plant.

BARBARA. *(Puzzled.)* What do you mean— you didn't tell me everything?

(FRED looks at her for a moment, stands, and moves to MILDRED.)

FRED. Yes— well there's another reason I don't want to move.

MILDRED. Fred, maybe this isn't the time to—

MOVING

FRED. Yes, I think it is, dear. *(To BARBARA.)* See, it's Mildred.
BARBARA. *(Not understanding.)* Mildred?
FRED. We're lovers.

(BARBARA stares at him for a long moment.)

BARBARA. *(Finally.)* You're— what?
FRED. Lovers.

(It occurs to BARBARA that FRED has slipped over into senility and she looks questioningly at Mildred.)

BARBARA. Is he—? *(She sees by MILDRED's face that he is telling the truth.)* You're—
FRED. Lovers.
MILDRED. I think there may be a better word to describe our relationship, Fred.
FRED. I know. I just like saying it.

(BARBARA, who is having enormous problems absorbing this information, tries to pull herself together.)

BARBARA. *(Disoriented.)* Wait a minute— how long— has this been going on?
FRED. Oh, longer than I can remember.
MILDRED. Eight years. We started as friends, Mrs. Hartman, and then it slowly ripened into something else.
BARBARA. *(Dully.)* Something else?
FRED. Yes. Of course the sex part's not as important as it used to be. *(He puts his arm around MILDRED.)* Now it's more a matter of — of sociability. *(Curiously.)* Didn't you ever suspect anything?
BARBARA. *(Still stunned.)* No— no, I didn't.

FRED. Didn't my behavior seem odd?
BARBARA. Odd? In what way?
FRED. Didn't you wonder why I never dated?

(BARBARA just stares at him.)

MILDRED. I know how you must feel, Mrs. Hartman. We're not exactly a match made in heaven. I mean we were aware of the differences between us.
FRED. Yes, Mildred's quite a few years younger than me. We seriously considered all the obstacles— I mean we're not kids— but love is a great destroyer of logic.
BARBARA. Love? What are you talking about? *(BARBARA, searching for some sanity in the situation, turns to MILDRED.)* Mildred—
MILDRED. I'm sorry, Mrs. Hartman, but—

(She takes FRED's hands, gazes into his eyes. They make a slightly comic but very touching picture.)

HARRY. *(Offstage.)* It wasn't just the piano.

(The three move into the living room. JOEY and JENNIFER are also present.)

HARRY. *(Continued.)* It wasn't just the piano.

(Everybody turns to look up at him.)

FRED. What?
HARRY. I want you to know it wasn't just losing the piano that made me fall apart.

MOVING

JOEY. It wasn't?

HARRY. No. It was when they took the running boards off cars.

(A small pause as they react.)

JOEY. Look, Pop, maybe you should lie down again until—

HARRY. No, I'm okay. But I feel I owe you all an explanation, *(He moves down the stairs during the following.)* It started when they took the running boards off cars. *(He sits on an empty packing case.)* Why did they do that? They looked good— you could sit on them— stand on them. Do you know what I'm trying to say?

FRED. That cars used to be better?

HARRY. I'm saying that everything used to be better. Hotels— newspapers— books— movies— food— am I lying? *(Glumly.)* Then when I dropped the piano I realized I used to be better.

JOEY. Anybody can drop a piano, Pop.

HARRY. Not me. Me dropping a piano is like— is like—

(He searches for a comparison.)

JOEY. Baryshnikov dropping a prima ballerina.

HARRY. *(Blankly.)* What?

FRED. Willie Hays dropping a pop up fly.

HARRY. *(This he understands.)* Yeah. Look, all my life I been in a business where I watched people move— uproot their lives. Every day I saw them lose their roots— their sense of— of community. I didn't like it but it was okay because everything else in my life stayed the same— at least the important things— my business, my marriage, my family. But then my wife died— my kids grew up— and my business started to come apart. So I looked around for the other things in life I used to cling to— other anchors, you know? But then I found even those had changed. You know what I'm saying?

(MILDRED speaks for the first time.)

   MILDRED. Stop grieving, Mr. Picardo.

(He turns to look at her.)

   HARRY. For my wife?
   MILDRED. For your youth. We all have to move on.
   HARRY. Look, do me a favor, will you? Don't tell me there's a
season for everything.
   MILDRED. Well, there is.
   HARRY. I know that. I just happen to like Spring!
   MILDRED. You have no choice, Mr. Picardo. Accept it.
   HARRY. Accept what?
   MILDRED. Life.
   HARRY. You know something? Maybe I should start going to
your church.
   MILDRED. You feeling happier?
   HARRY. More accepting. Maybe it's the same thing.

(JENNIFER nudges JOEY who approaches his father.)

   JOEY. Pop, there's something I have to tell you.
   HARRY. What is it, Joey?
   JOEY. I want to leave the business and become a ballet dancer.

(A small pause.)

   HARRY. Okay, kid, if that's what you really want.
   JOEY. *(Surprised.)* You don't mind.

MOVING

HARRY. It's your life. You deserve a shot.

JOEY. I'll still be able to work part-time for you. And Jenny can fill in for me.

HARRY. Jenny?

JOEY. She's a great mechanic, Pop. She could get the other two trucks going and keep them rolling. And she can drive for you too. She's real strong so she can even help with the loading.

HARRY. Whatever you say, kid.

JOEY. Thanks, Pop. And there's one other thing.

HARRY. Yeah?

JOEY. I'm also gay.

(A long pause.)

HARRY. You think I didn't know that?

JOEY. *(Stunned.)* You did?

HARRY. I'm your old man for god's sake. You think a father wouldn't know a thing like that about his kid?

JOEY. And you don't mind talking about it?

HARRY. Of course I mind talking about it. That's why I haven't talked about it. Anyway, what's to talk about?

JOEY. I just thought —

HARRY Look, Joey, is there any way I can talk you out of this?

JOEY No.

HARRY So I know and you know I know and that should be enough. I accept it, okay?

JOEY. Okay, Pop.

(He starts towards the door.)

HARRY. Joey? *(JOEY turns.)* If you want we'll talk about it later, kid.

MOVING

(JOEY moves down the stairs, embraces his father, and then EXITS with JENNIFER. HARRY looks over to MILDRED who is smiling.)

MILDRED. I'm glad you accept it, Harry.

HARRY. Look, I accept it, okay! I accept it! Don't bug me!

MILDRED. This is you accepting?

HARRY. I'm Italian! We act this way! We yell about things that don't matter anymore so we don't have to dwell on stuff that does matter!

MILDRED. What's that, Harry?

HARRY. That is my last moving job!

FRED. Why? Jenny can—

HARRY. It's got nothing to do with Jenny— or Joey— it's got to do with me. Don't you get it? When I lost that piano I also lost my nerve and when a moving man's lost his nerve he may as well hang up his steel hooks. *(To MILDRED.)* You got anything to say that can fix that?

MILDRED. No.

(At this point, MAVIS, the real estate woman, bustles in.)

MAVIS. Mrs. Hartman, I've been sitting in that car for over an hour. What have you decided?

(HARRY turns, notices BARBARA for the first time.)

HARRY. *(Wearily.)* Yeah, what's it going to do, lady? Do we move or do we all go home?

BARBARA. I've decided —

MOVING

(But she doesn't finish the sentence as TIMMY, his clothes in some disarray, and almost incoherent, rushes onto the landing from upstairs.)

TIMMY. Mom— something's— happened. Lisa and I were in— in Hilary's old room in the closet and—

BARBARA. What were you doing in the closet?

TIMMY. Uh— packing— and we heard this yelling and— and groaning from the room and— and when we came out of the—

BARBARA. All right, slow down, Timmy. What is it? Slowly.

TIMMY. *(Slowly.)* Hilary— is— having— a baby.

BARBARA. *(Puzzled.)* I know that, dear.

TIMMY. I mean now!

BARBARA. She's — she's gone into labor?

TIMMY. No. She's having a baby! She said to tell you. She's yelling and having a baby in her room!

BARBARA. Oh, my God. *(She pulls herself together.)* Timmy, call a doctor— No, find your father and tell him to phone Doctor Ballyntine. The number's by the phone. Then get him to phone the hospital. Go on! *(She starts upstairs.)* Jenny!

(TIMMY rushes down the stairs and outside as JENNIFER runs upstairs.)

BARBARA. *(Continued.)* Jenny, go and get the car started.

(BARBARA EXITS upstairs as JENNIFER runs out of the house. Picardo turns to MILDRED.)

HARRY. You ever delivered a baby, Mildred?

MILDRED. Only when I was under an anesthetic.

HARRY. Better unpack some clean towels. You never know.

MOVING

MILDRED. How come you're such an expert?

HARRY. Before I got into the moving business I used to be a cab driver.

(As MILDRED moves to search for some towels and TIMMY and CHARLIE quickly ENTER and CHARLIE moves to phone and frantically dials. A very distraught BARBARA rushes onto the landing.)

BARBARA. Mildred, we're not going to make it! We need your help!

MILDRED. *(Indicating HARRY.)* Better talk to Doctor Kildare here.

BARBARA What?

HARRY. *(Panicky.)* Wait a minute! That was years ago. I can't—

MILDRED. Harry, this is no time to start acting like Butterfly MeQueen.

HARRY. But—

BARBARA. *(Imploring.)* Mr. Picardo— please!

HARRY. Okay— okay, I'll— I'll do the best I can. I'll— I'll try.

(He lumbers up the stairs, trips.)

BARBAR A. Are you going to make it?

HARRY. Yes— and don't worry, Mrs. Hartman. Everything's going to be all right.

BARBARA. *(Hopefully.)* It is?

HARRY. Yeah. *(He pulls himself to his full height.)* I never dropped a baby in my life!

(MILDRED and BARBARA exchange horrified looks. CROSSFADE

MOVING

TO: It is a few hours later, twilight, and BARBARA is sitting on the steps of the gazebo. CHARLIE comes out of the house.)

CHARLIE. You okay?

BARBARA. Just wondering how much you tip someone who delivers your grandson in perfect shape.

CHARLIE. I think making him the godfather is more than sufficient. Made a new man of him.

BARBARA. How you doing granddad?

CHARLIE. Granddad. I'd only just got used to having the car on Saturday night.

BARBARA. I know. It seems a minute ago we met and how — *(she snaps her fingers.)*— grandparents.

CHARLIE. Yeah. It's been a sweet ride though, hasn't it, kid?

BARBARA. Yes.

(She sits beside him.)

CHARLIE. So what do you say, my love? You want to grow old with me?

BARBARA. Is there any way you can make that sound a little more exciting?

CHARLIE. Oh, I'm sure there'll be a few laughs along the way. If you promise to provide the straight lines.

BARBARA. Are you sure that's what you want?

CHARLIE. Of course. What makes you ask?

BARBARA. *(A small shrug.)* Emotional day. Moving makes everyone crazy.

CHARLIE. Us getting back together in this house is the least crazy idea I ever had. *(A beat.)* Don't you still love me, kid?

BARBARA. *(With almost a hint of regret.)* Oh, yes.

CHARLIE. What is it then? Can't forgive me?

MOVING

(She gets up, moves away, thinks for a moment.)

BARBARA. Charlie, would you move to Albuquerque with me?

CHARLIE. *(Thrown.)* What — what would I do out there? Write commercials for the Pony Express?

BARBARA. I don't know. Every so often, to survive, you have to reinvent yourself. Part of the burden of living in America.

CHARLIE. I've tried reinventing myself. I just can't do it without roots.

BARBARA. You won't come?

CHARLIE. I'm sorry, honey. I— I just can't.

BARBARA. *(Finally— with regret.)* That's too bad.

CHARLIE. That's— it?

BARBARA. I'm— afraid so.

CHARLIE. Barbara, why don't you save yourself a lot of pain. Believe me— I've been out there.

BARBARA. I know. But I have to try.

CHARLIE. Why?

BARBARA. I don't want to die— wondering.

CHARLIE. May I ask you again in a year?

BARBARA. *(Gently.)* Only if I don't ask you first.

(They look at one another for a moment before he heads for the house. At the door he turns.)

CHARLIE. Barbara?

(She looks at him.)

CHARLIE. *(Continued.)* Always remember who loved you first, huh?

MOVING

(Her eyes brimming, she nods. He EXITS. Left alone, BARBARA slowly sits and we see how much the decision has cost her. Her mood is shattered as Mavis, holding real estate papers, EN-TERS.)

MAVIS. Your husband said you wanted to see me.

BARBARA. *(Disoriented.)* What? Oh yes— I'm ready to sign those papers now.

MAVIS. Hallelujah!

(She quickly moves to give BARBARA the papers. BARBARA is just about to sign when FRED and MILDRED ENTER from the house.)

MILDRED. Mrs. Hartman, before you sign those, Fred and I have something to say.

BARBARA. Mildred, can it wait until —

FRED. No, it can't, Barbara. You'd better listen to her.

(BARBARA looks up from forms. FRED turns to MILDRED.)

FRED. *(Continued.)* Go ahead, my dear.

MILDRED. Well, I've been working for families in this neighborhood almost all my life. I've worked in this house alone for close to thirty-five years.

MAVIS. Look, could you just skip to the highlights?

MILDRED. As you know, I have six kids and I needed something else— some business on the side to make ends meet.

BARBARA. What sort of business?

MILDRED. Well, over the years, people I worked for gave me things. You know how families pass on odds and ends to their maids— things they have no use for anymore. Well, I just kept storing things up and about twenty years ago I started selling them out of my backyard. You know, sort of a small junkyard.

BARBARA. *(Puzzled.)* That's— that's very nice, Mildred, but—

MILDRED. Then a few years ago I found out that some people didn't think of yesterday's odds and ends as junk. They thought of them as antiques. That's when I opened the shop.

BARBARA. An antique shop?

FRED. *(Proudly.)* And thriving. Mildred's built a very nice future for herself by restoring and selling pieces of the past.

MILDRED. Well, it's a family business really. All my children work in the shop. We've done okay.

BARBARA. *(Puzzled.)* I'm pleased to hear that, Mildred, but I still don't understand why you're telling me all this now.

MILDRED. Mrs. Hartman, all my kids still live at home. Two of them are married with kids of their own so the place is bursting at the seams. Anyway, while we were waiting for Hilary's baby to be born, Fred and me came up with an idea.

FRED. I told her about the money I had put aside.

MILDRED. We did some figuring and between the two of us we think we can scrape enough together to buy this place from you.

BARBARA. You want to buy this house?

FRED. We could fill every room, Barbara. Of course I'd stay here with Mildred and Hilary could keep her old room and raise the baby. Even when she's ready to work again she'd never have to hire a sitter and—

MAVIS. Wait a minute! What are you talking about? You can't move into this house!

MILDRED. Why not?

MAVIS. You're black!

MILDRED. Really?

MAVIS. I mean this neighborhood's always been lily white.

MOVING

People won't stand for it.

MILDRED. Of course it would only be fair to pay you a commission on the sale.

MAVIS. *(Without a beat.)* On the other hand — times change.

FRED. What do you say, daughter?

(Before she can answer HARRY PICARDO comes out of the house.)

HARRY. We're all waiting, Mrs. Hartman. What's the word?

(BARBARA looks from one to the other.)

BARBARA. *(Finally— joyfully.)* Roll 'em!

(BARBARA moves to embrace MILDRED. The living room is empty except for one large packing case. It begins to shake and then stops. The top is pushed open and LISA and TIMMY, flushed and triumphant, emerge. They kiss and EXIT hand in hand. BARBARA and CHARLIE ENTER, meet on the landing, come down the stairs, look around the empty room and then at each other.)

BARBARA. *(Continued.)* Thank you, Charlie.

CHARLIE. For what?

BARBARA. Polishing up some tarnished memories.

(He nods in understanding, moves to front door and EXITS. BARBARA takes a last look around, puts her hand to her mouth, blows the house a gentle kiss and EXITS. The stage is empty. The CURTAIN SLOWLY FALLS and the play is over.)

THE END

Late Flowering
JOHN CHAPMAN and IAN DAVIDSON

These masters of uproarious comedy have created another delightfully funny cast of characters. Constance Beauchamp, an elegant spinster, runs a marriage bureau for the well-to-do in a fashionable area of London. She is assisted by a hard-working secretary who is set in her ways and happy with her old-fashioned filing system. Constance insists on installing a computer. The man who comes to teach them how to use it is an odd-ball bachelor who decides to feed in his own profile through the machine to find an ideal mate. After some hilarious trials and errors, Constance is alarmed to discovers it's her! 1 m., 4 f. (#13834)

The Trouble with Trent
FRED CARMICHAEL

Sparkling dialogue and laughs galore abound in this tale of mistaken identities that begins when three mystery buffs who become acquainted on the Internet E-mail chapters to each other and meet for two weeks to polish off their first book. Book sales soar when their agent hints that Sarah Trent, the pen name they use, is a real person. Meanwhile, a Washington socialite being blackmailed intends to send Sarah a story she has written about herself. She mistakenly sends the manuscript to the blackmailer and the payoff money to the three ladies behind the name Trent who have gathered to write another book. Government agents pursuing the blackmailer and a man claiming to be Mr. Trent are just two of the people who pop up. This is first-rate comedy by the popular author of numerous widely produced plays. 2 m., 6 f. (#22744)

**Send for your copy of the Samuel French
BASIC CATALOGUE OF PLAYS AND MUSICALS**